BURNT OFFERINGS

BURNT
OFFERINGS

*

Timothy Liu

COPPER CANYON PRESS

Publication of this book is supported by a grant from the National
Endowment for the Arts and a grant from the Lannan Foundation.
Additional support to Copper Canyon Press has been provided by the
Andrew W. Mellon Foundation, the Lila Wallace–Reader's Digest
Fund, and the Washington State Arts Commission. Copper Canyon
Press is in residence with Centrum at Fort Worden State Park.

Library of Congress Cataloging-in-Publication Data
Liu, Timothy.
Burnt Offerings / Timothy Liu.
        p.   cm.
ISBN 1-55659-104-7 (pbk.)
1. Gay men – Poetry. 2. Erotic poetry, American. 1. Title.
PS3562.1799B87   1995
811.'54 – dc20   95-32454

9 8 7 6 5 4 3 2 1

COPPER CANYON PRESS
P.O. BOX 271, PORT TOWNSEND, WASHINGTON, 98368

ACKNOWLEDGMENTS

The poems in this book first appeared in the following publications: *Caliban*, *Harvard Review*, *Kenyon Review*, *Massachusetts Review*, *Paris Review*, *Poetry East*, *positions: east asia cultures critique*, *Provincetown Arts*, *The Quarterly*, *Quarterly West*, *Western Humanities Review*, *Willow Springs* and *Yellow Silk*.

For their friendship and support during the writing of this book, I would like to thank Bruce Beasley, Christopher Davis, Linda Gregg, Richard Howard, Jane Mead, Pamela Stewart, Jean Valentine, and Michael White. *Bello in allegra vampa svanir!*

CONTENTS

IV.

For Christopher James Arabadjis

BURNT OFFERINGS

INVOCATION

I call upon you, voice forbidden
from the beginning, a sibylline spell to summon
a god – that o-shaped flume descending
into breath's dark furnace…
To speak in cycles of the moon, desire
thrusting upward through the hole that silence is:
how the world was filled with one sound
that splintered into the many selves we call a soul,
endless babble in the mouth of an old woman
confined to a chair on wheels –

> *Where am I going? Where am I*
> *going? I am sitting here*
> *getting older and older…*

She reads no further. Outside,
children sled down hills she can no longer climb
while notes from an upright piano
drift out the window – *so meaningless*, she thinks,
this hour, this music, this snow…
Or was it a dream repeating itself
through a life that escaped her attention –
an atrium of twilight where the blind are gathered,
hands groping down spiral banisters
as they ease themselves past memory's double doors.

I.

ECHOES

The world exists again. The roses drop their petals
from the railing of a ship and we wave goodbye.
An open hand is a hand letting go of flowers
in all their freshness, memory pressed into a diary
sinking to the bottom of the sea. All my life
the sound I've been trying to hear is the sound
of my own voice. I thirst in full view of the ocean
that lies before me. We are not swimmers, taciturn,
sipping tea without a twist of lemon. Outside,
the shadows in the orchard have merged into night.

*

I cannot help it, going on like this, the windows
turning colder by the hour. Once I was seduced
by the sibilance of tires in the rain while staring
into my coffee at a vacant diner. An oldie
on the jukebox made me cry, not words I never learned
but that voice which took me back to a summer flat
in Taipei, laundry sweating out of open windows.
I was two years old in a tub, Ah-poh singing,
her hands playful as porpoises. I would only cry
if Mother came to finish the job, tepid water
slapping all around as she scoured my genitals.
Whenever I hear a baby scream, I gag its mouth
to keep it quiet, just the way I want it.

*

When I turned seven, I made Ian lie down
on the bathroom floor, next to a crowded kitchen
where our mothers were rolling meat-filled

dumplings, dropping them into smoking grease.
I hummed a tune to calm him down, unzipping
his pants in order to rescue his penis
from a house on fire, that sole survivor we dressed
in strips of gauze. Later I felt the way you do
when spoiling a gift by unwrapping it too soon.
Still, I got what I wanted by taking on new roles –
a captain, a pirate, a preacher who promised
to forget the whole thing when it was over.
Only Cathy wouldn't shut up, even after I had run
my fingers over the flowers on her underpants
while pinning her down: *You're going to have a baby*.
Somebody had already dealt another hand
of bridge, each parent holding a fan of cards
with sailboats on them, when Cathy came out crying,
I'm going to have a baby, and to my relief,
all I heard was her voice drowning in their laughter.

*

I have heard that oldie blaring out from windows
of a passing car, from a beat-up radio lost
in a janitor's closet. There's this church
I would pass on my way to school but never enter.
It's like that, each of us minding our own business,
then one day we are called. Phone soliciting
was not my pick for a first job, but it opened doors:
*Hello. I'm with the San Jose Symphony. Subscribe
tonight and win a free cruise*. Over and over,
my adolescent echo down a reverse directory
until that voice: *Ever wanted a dick in your mouth?*
I've learned to say no, but then it was only yes,
yes to those lips moving across the face of the deep.

*

Sometimes it seems I cry for no reason, trying
to convince myself that I am still here. I draw
a square on my palm and say this is a prison
where we are born. Each day the walls grow more
transparent. The night of Jessye Norman's recital,
we stood up when she sang "He's Got the Whole World
in His Hands" for her final encore, our applause
shattering across the stage like glass roses,
her smile roaring through the hall as she sailed
into the wings, waving goodbye. It was over,
our voices released as if from an old Victrola
spinning on the ocean floor, each of us breathless
in that echo of the lives we have loved and lost.

THOREAU

My father and I have no place to go.
His wife will not let us in the house –
afraid of catching AIDS. She thinks
sleeping with men is more than a sin,
my father says, as we sit on the curb
in front of someone else's house.
Sixty-four years have made my father
impotent. Silver roots, faded black
dye mottling his hair make him look
almost comical, as if his shame
belonged to me. Last night we read
Thoreau in a steak house down the road
and wept: *If a man does not keep pace*
with his companions, let him travel
to the music that he hears, however
measured or far away. The orchards
are gone, his village near Shanghai
bombed by the Japanese, the groves
I have known in Almaden – apricot,
walnut, peach and plum – hacked down.

THE SIZE OF IT

I knew the length of an average penis
    was five to seven inches, a fact
I learned upstairs in the stacks marked 610
    or HQ, not down in the basement
where I knelt behind a toilet stall, waiting
    for eight-and-a-half inches or more
to fill my mouth with a deeper truth. The heart
    grows smaller, like a cut rose drying
in the sun. Back then I was only fourteen,
    with four-and-three-quarters inches
at full erection. I began equating
    Asian with inadequate, unable
to compete with others in the locker room
    after an icy swim (a shriveled
bud between my fingers as I tried to shake
    some semblance of life back into it).
Three times a day, I jacked off faithfully, yet
    nothing would enlarge my future, not
ads for vacuum pumps, nor ancient herbs. Other
    men had to compensate, one billion
Chinese measured against what? Some said my cock
    had a classical shape, and I longed
for the ruins of Greece. Others took it up
    the ass, reassuring in their way,
yet nothing helped me much on my knees at night
    praying one more inch would make me whole.

READING WHITMAN IN A TOILET STALL

A security-man who stood, arms crossed, outside
the men's room (making sure that no one lingered)
met my eyes with the same dispassionate gaze as
a woman inside, kneeling to clean the toilets.

The faintly buzzing flicker of fluorescent light
erased the contours of a place where strangers
openly parade their sex. Efficient, silent,
all ammonia and rubber gloves, she was in and

out of there in minutes, taking no notice
of the pocket Whitman that I leafed my way through
before the others arrived. *In paths untrodden, /*
In the growth by margins of pondwaters, / Escaped

from the light that exhibits itself – how those words
came flooding back to me while men began to take
their seats, glory holes the size of silver dollars
in the farthest stall where no adolescent went

unnoticed. O daguerreotyped Walt, your collar
unbuttoned, hat lopsided, hand on hip, your sex
never evading our view! how we are confined
by steel partitions, dates and initials carved

into the latest coat of paint, an old car key
the implement of our secret desires. *Wanted:*
uncut men with lots of cheese. No fats. No femmes.
Under twenty a real plus. How each of us must

learn to decipher the erotic hieroglyphs
of our age, prayers on squares of one-ply paper
flushed daily down the john where women have knelt
in silence, where men with folded arms stand guard

while we go about our task, our tongues made holy
by licking each other's asshole clean, shock of sperm
warm in our mouths, white against the clothes we wear
as we walk out of our secrets into the world.

HIGHWAY 6

A caravan heading east on Highway 6
with muscled men whose eyes are flashing
neon in a world of vacancy signs –
a Day-Glo decal shining on the window of a car
pulled off the side of the road, buzzards
lodged in pines with evening in their wings.
To love the moon in Provincetown as salt
glistens on the skin of shirtless men
cruising down Commercial Street, hand in hand,
as if death were merely some erotic aftertaste.
We are tethered to what we own, a ring
of keys with a different name engraved on each,
the doors we have locked now creaking open
not fifty miles from here. How memory's brake
locks up like a car spinning out on ice
while thirty birds on a wire all fly up at once.
Already I can hear the tow trucks revving up
their engines, trash bags in a moonlit ditch
filled with genitals, a full set of fingertips
last seen on a man who was leaving town
in the plush interior of a stranger's car –
guesthouse lights floating near the water line
where dead fish wash ashore, a cloud of birds
turning in to roost at the deserted harbor.
What would it matter now if a pair of headlights
suddenly swerved – and the world vanished.

WELLFLEET

Our last resort. Lovers wading back to shore
with ankles garlanded in ropes of kelp,
my hand poised over notebooks that refuse
to close. On the horizon, a single sail
blazes late into the afternoon, the hours
receding without a sound. Wild rosehips
scattered along the beach while sandwiches
on sterile trays are wheeled past rooms
for the sick. Mother, no more mattresses
floating out to sea, nor ashes in urns,
the waves all sliding in well-oiled grooves
that heave up wakes of trash – shrieking
gulls circling above those watery graves.

CHATHAM

So many doors through which New England disappears.
No safety here amid Bed & Breakfast Bibles
pilfered from our drawers, Dante's Nineteenth Canto
buried in a thrift shop behind the local church –
the feet of Blake's inverted man bursting to flames.

Nothing else changes, only flowers rearranged
near calendars hung on rusty nails, holy days
discarded by immaculate maids like tinder
for the fire – the town's off-season stillness akin
to that lighthouse etched in stone above our twin beds.

WINTER

How long will the bed that we made together
hold us there? Your stubbled cheeks grazed my skin
from evening to dawn, a cloud of scattered
particles now, islands of shaving foam
slowly spiraling down the drain, blood drops
stippling the water pink as I kiss
the back of your neck, our faces framed inside
a medicine cabinet mirror. The blade
of your hand carves a portal out of steam,
the two of us like boys behind frosted glass
who wave goodbye while a car shoves off
into winter. All that went unnoticed
till now – empty cups of coffee stacked up
in the sink, the neighborhood kids
up to their necks in mounds of autumn leaves.
How months on a kitchen calendar drop
like frozen flies, the flu season at its peak
followed by a train of magic-markered
xxx's – nights we'd spend apart. Death must work
that way, a string of long distance calls
that only gets through to the sound of your voice
on our machine, my heart's mute confession
screened out. How long before we turn away
from flowers altogether, your blind hand
reaching past our bedridden shoulders
to hit that digital alarm at delayed
intervals – till you shut it off completely.

FORTY-PERCENT CHANCE OF RAIN

The water in your flower vase five days old,
my radio losing its signal as the sky
draws near. Or is it fear of dying alone
that moves us toward each other in this room,
petals falling on a Bible marked in red.
Only static hiss from a local station
comforts us, signing off in a still small voice
that echoes in our bones, a moon now painting
the side of a broken bed where our faces
grow too heavy for us to lift, and the room
we share starts sinking into the ground.

II.

WITH CHAOS IN EACH KISS

Outside your door, an ocean
of violets, wave upon wave, so many petals
torn by the wind and rain.
                                    I stood there waiting
until the door opened onto a room
that held a few chairs
                                    and a grand piano,
floral paper cutouts framed under glass
hanging at eye level,
                                    a gold-leaf print
with a solitary boat not sailing on water
but its absence.
                                    For hours we spoke of music,
a score of *Don Quixote* on the table,
a song slowly composing itself inside my body –

(the two of us anchored to our chairs
as we sat facing opposite walls)

and I thought of our hands that labor
for beauty yet unknown to the world,
a calendar of empty hours
                                    suddenly filled
with birds and fields of wildflowers,
an oversized violin left out in the sun.

                    *

You start to reach for my hand
as we part, desire a place

where we can rest, our hands
driving the darkest horses

across a thundering field
where no human voice returns.

*

The other instruments faded
months after Ginastera's *Variation for Viola*
while your strings continued to echo
in the concert hall I dreamed, pure music
exploding from a hive of bees.
                        There is a gulf
that separates reality from desire.
You stood there with a viola made of glass,
the rows of velvet chairs between us
a river I refused to cross, not knowing
which way to turn –
                        if only you had reached
into that churning sea of faces before
the music once again began.

*

Our voices would take the place of music.
Near the window, a piano with its lid

propped open like a yawn, our watches
ticking on. For hours I had stood outside

your studio listening to all the notes.
When you asked me in, I was too afraid

to ask you for a song, my ear still red
from pressing hard against the door.

     *

When I heard another voice on your machine,
I knew you had been unfaithful
to your music, turning towards human love
instead of a god.
             It was then I saw an open grave
with three men kneeling at the edge looking in,
unable to lie down in that silence.
                 Unquiet hearts –
why do the houses that we build in time
become our prisons, as if our beds were not
a place to rest? And why was there a ring
of keys glittering at the bottom of that grave?

     *

Not asking to see the room
where you and your lover
sleep or wake (the city
we share will be enough)
nor the walls that hold

your shadow, the sunrise
igniting an open window
where you pull up a chair
and begin to rehearse
in that unprofaned hour.

*

Since that night when you first held me
hostage against a body seasoned
with seven faithful years of marriage,
all my minutes now are filled
with longing. I did not know
what you had freely given
would cost me in the end, your hands
behind my back like thieves whispering:
we do not know what we are doing.

*

Nothing is easy about this love.
Not the marriages we carry
in our hearts like dry corsages.

There is an ocean within my body
I cannot contain, a history
twisting upward in broken columns

as merchant ships at last reach
harbor, bringing flowers and news
of you, bell of my body ringing

under arches that have not fallen
while roses perfume the world
with the splendor of their dying.

*

I slept alone. Only the voices of dead singers
kept me company. When you first held me,
I told you I was sad – not meaning then
but all my life. We stood there like a world
that had no words. Now the cats are crying
to be fed, but I do not rise. All I can do
is dream about that field where I had knelt
cutting wildflowers to leave outside your door.

*

*I do not ask for summer roses
when your body is near. Nor a gown
the bride has outgrown. Love me
not as a wife but as the stray cat
who sleeps on your chest each night.*

*I who am poor at heart surrender
to your shirts, that unearthly
flower of desire opening whenever
you are near, a joy that lingers
in the room long after you have gone.*

*

Memory is not the doll that gets left
behind when the house catches fire.
Nor that photo you returned, the one
where I am six, holding a Siamese cat
named Mimi now buried in that backyard
where I stood. You should have kept it –
love is not less because of loss.

This morning I am listening to a tape
of Hindemith's *Trauermusik*, your viola
the closest I can get to the voice
of sadness that is always singing
beneath the visible.

How antique clocks
have endured our deepest longings –
an unheard music winding through
our daily routines without reprieve.

Where was I that summer when crowds
began to applaud as you walked on stage?
Only a notebook entry: *May get to walk
by the river tomorrow.*
All that time
I had closed my eyes while the orchestra
performed Rachmaninov's *Symphonic Dances.*
Later you would ask if I somehow knew
the part that reminded you of Chekhov:

*Anna Sergeyevna seemed to regard the affair
as something very special, very serious,
as if she had become a fallen woman.*

A critic said that the piece would run
more smoothly if that part were cut out,
the only measures that mattered –
not the saxophone off-tune – the viola
at rest in your lap, you sitting there
on stage, me in the dark, the two of us
listening to all that there was between us.

        *

Without love, I should remain
a ghost that wanders the earth
looking for fire that burns for me
in the corner of someone's eyes –

How can the ocean continue to sing
if all of our strings are broken,
if there is no place on this earth
where we can lie down for an hour?

*

Hour after hour, they arrive
at your door, unable to explain
the distance practice can create
in a room that has become
too intimate, duty and beauty
caught between the steady swings
of a metronome keeping time.

You ask me why I think of death.
I have no answers, only flowers
that have not finished their song –
all day long you gaze at them
while your students labor
to bring music into the world.

And when they finally get it right
in that hour that has turned
ethereal with what we cannot share,
do you forget that what is given
to lift the soul out of sadness
can only last in that moment
when all that we love holds still?

*

Without fear, love would lie still,
cadaverous, unable to throw a ring
of keys across the room.
                    Or cry out
in a sculpture garden where nothing
but beauty reigns.
                    Never enough
time for us to lay our bodies down
across a stone bench.
                    Or feel the sun
renew a flower with possibility
even as honeybees empty chambers
of all their sweetness.
                    What we want
is the drone of a hive as it begins
to swarm, a storm of transparent wings
in the season's uncertain crescendo —

that litany across a mellifluous sky.

*

Each dawn comes to me like a burning violin.
The dirge that starts the day issues from s-shaped
gashes in the sky even as the dogwood blooms
outside, stigmata on each petal punctuating time.
Like Isaac on his father's back, you carried me
up the mountainside, but I was not willing to die.
Isaac surrendered to the will of heaven, not saying
a word. In Rembrandt's *The Sacrifice of Isaac*,
the hand of Abraham covers his son's entire face,
no pain to be seen in Abraham's face, no hesitation,
no sign that he is conscious. But I must speak.
For in every wound there is a truth, a revelation
like a ram caught in a thicket, each brush stroke
on the canvas obedient to a law I cannot live.
I woke up crying, *what shall I do with my life?*,
fearing the paralysis of each hour until I heard
your voice: *I need you the way that I need music.*
It was then I knew. Only love can make us visible.

*

You rest with your partner, eager
to tidy up the nest and welcome

another dawn. I try to imagine
each kiss not meant for me, each

caress, the words I long to hear
on a tongue I pray still burns

*for me, though I can no longer feel
it in my mouth, now empty, no song –*

only a phoenix rising with a shriek.

*

There is only one path, the one
that you're on, happiness
in your own hands
and not in someone else's.
Death said, *Wait*
and I will give you rest.
Death said, *Later*
and you shall belong to me.
But water was running
over the path, and I was swept away.

*

*I slept. A white room with an ocean
painted on all four walls, a cradle
rocking on the center of a cold floor.
An infant crying out your name –
Horses dashed into the void, lovers
singing notes off key on a bridge
that stretched across an empty sea.*

*

Your sudden retreat left me useless,
horizontal, unable to let go of the future
or the past: two roses on the dashboard
with a straight pin stuck through each.
What I wore on my lapel you hid away,
taste of my cock still fresh in your mouth,
me almost naked on a music room floor.
Your mind was already racing halfway home
with a can of chicken broth – to nurse
your partner back to health for all the guilt
you felt – *that would always be your story.*
Now my heart is filled with Marguerite
imploring Faust to dig two graves, not three,
your viola lost among Boito's pure lament.
Forgive me for tasting Christ in your blood
that cried out from your diabetic veins,
a secret you kept for fear of impotence
and shame, taking no thought for tomorrow
while our anxious hearts created a world
in the cab of my truck, in the backseat
of your flooded car, the rain coming down
in sheets across Houston's concrete skyline,
all concerts canceled in that brief bliss
of calamity that passed with the weather,
water under the bridge. Forgive me –
we were only human with chaos in each kiss.

*

In a world of endless pleasures,
why did I keep looking for you
while words kept falling out
of all my books? Why did I want
to become your final pleasure
while tankards of beer spilled
over? There was music left
unheard, unveiled sculptures
that would have made you frown
if you had known how I waited
to look at you, you who deny
your own face. How have I become
this man who fell in love
with less and less? What lie
did I swallow that the world
should hide its face from me
and trees hold on to their leaves
instead of letting go.

III.

IKON

Nothing comforts me, not Gloria Swanson
in a black-and-white toque, nor Colette
reclining on a red divan, her chin at rest
near the edge of a table with flowers on it.
No matter where I stand, spindled postcards
in an all-night diner, tins of custard pie
vanishing from the counter while faces
come alive, mercy in the sound of quarters
being dropped into a jukebox. The songs I know
but cannot sing remind me of a stranger
who undid my khaki trousers in the back
of an eighteen-wheeler, who said he wanted
to fuck me with a crowbar while kissing
the face of Christ he kept inside his wallet.

SUNDAY

And when they sat down in the morning
to bowls of cold cereal, each in turn
would notice the blades of a ceiling fan
spinning at the bottom of their spoons,
small enough to swallow, yet no one
ever mentioned it, neither looking up
nor into each other's eyes for fear
of feeding the hunger that held them there.

THE ROAD TO SEDER

How my legs would have to carry me further
to the sign of water. An angel appeared
in a black robe. There were no wings,
only a parachute closing all around us
as though we were being carried away in a cloud.

The throne of God was a wheelchair of fire.
There was no God, only a pair of crutches
thrown down. A long way off, the sun
continued to turn in its vast confusion,
a spiral of souls floating past the mountain.

IN THE OUTHOUSE

He thrust his meat
down my throat, left me

     with a few words –
     beautiful husks,
     not butterflies

fluttering their wings
for the first time.

REST STOP, HIGHWAY 91

Cars parked alongside a chainlink fence
overlooking houses that have no view,
        plates from three bordering states aglow
                in the light from a hillside billboard
        filled with a glass of milk – Holyoke
just beyond the notch, slumbering
        like a rain-soaked paper on the porch –
                checkout boys from the local A&P
        hanging up their aprons, clocking out
on a night that is young only once
        in a stranger's car – the taste of skin
                on clandestine tongues, freckled swirls
        down creamy backs in constellations
left unnamed, stiff cocks under boxers
        crammed into that vinyl dark perfumed
                by a four-inch cardboard pine dangling
        above the illuminated dash, windows veiled
with frost. They say the leaves will fall
        earlier this year, like so many apples
                plastered on the hill, wooden barrels
        filling up with rain while children turn
in their sleep – deaf to the sound of engines
        running, their fathers behind the wheel.

WHITE MOTHS

          espaliered
to a radiator grille
or hurled
          from the glass cave
of a child's mason jar

into the garden spider's web –
a slow dance
          of paralytic
stings, death's handiwork

spun out of silk, cradled
by the wind –
          and the bodies
warm to touch in the rising

drone of dusk still flutter
among
          the bronzed backs
of men in the park –
                    pale wings
fanning a glitter of dust.

THE MARRIAGE

The season's leaves half over at their peak
as we drive down the hill. Or else we have
no darkness, no sentence to begin with –
marriage an engine full of mileage
while lovers wander naked through the woods
with Polaroids, close-ups of their faces
emerging from dark squares like Eurydice
just before Orpheus turned to look –

which is why I ask you to take me
from the rear, one hand choking my neck
with a silk scarf, the other clamping
down on my hip as you ride up and down
so hard on a motel bed our bodies
enter myth. And for the first time in years
I model for the charcoal lines you draw,
holding myself more still than breath allows –

and what shame there ever was comes
rushing back to inhabit whatever form
we can give to it. Let me chariot
your bones into the sun that crimsons
every leaf caught under these crude wheels –
a coarse rope taut against the harness
of delight, your muscled flanks that pull
desire's thread through the needle's eye –

I CAME

in your mouth and felt the season's first frost
spreading fast across every windshield in town,
each leaf surrendering its voice to a chorus
that swelled beneath the ground. Or was it death
asking you to kneel before the fountain of my groin
and drink in all of our days with parted lips
to the end of your desire? There were no words
in your mouth, only a river swiftly taking us down.

BREUGHEL

Hatchet marks in the trunk of a pine.
Winter cracking across that lake
where the ice fishers gather –
ashes and a burning coal.

What fire is this
that the ragged men who huddle there
now hold their hands out over it
like the apostles of old.

CELAN

He woke
each day
not knowing

which hour
would be
the worst,

then made
a grid
of language

out of ash –
learned not
to trust

his own
mother
tongue,

knowing
all along
how it

would turn
on him
in the end.

IV.

MANIFEST DESTINY

The gods of this new world
have no honor. A parrot shouts

Christ, perched on a widow's porch,
while dozens of its kind

are shoveled into a furnace. *Christ*.
A whistle blows its plume of smoke

across the land, train after train
pulling out of the empty stations.

A GRAVE

He was crying. *Somebody get his mother.*
All day the exhumed bodies in trash bags.

Men, women, dogs. Even a parakeet
under a cross made of popsicle sticks

with a name written on it. Not the meat.
The bones the children leave after eating.

NUDE FIGURE DANCING
IN THE FOREGROUND

You walk into a room where the women gather,
knitting stockings others will grow into.
Nothing comforts like the steady clicking
of needles. Ecclesiastes said there is
a time for all things. I only want to know
the final pattern, the right fit. What if
we dance in an autumn field where the moon
is nowhere to be found? The women gone
to their beds leave lamb's wool by the fire,
everything coming undone, dogs racing
into the heart of their immaculate rooms.

SURVIVORS

Some mornings I do not hear
the alarm go off. The lightest
touch will startle me awake,
filling our bedroom with cries
of birds. It's not the hours
spent in therapy, nor self-
help books stacked beside our bed,
that keep me up until four
each night – it's your body
reeking of alcohol. Hold me
like a dream that will dissolve,
a childhood you never had.
Go on sleeping while I count
fifty dollar bills floating
up the chimney, black sheep
without a shepherd. It's not God
we trust, but ash, spindled
faces that never cracked a smile.

MEN WITHOUT

My father is a coward, and I have grown
to love the man who took my hand, afraid
of leaving my side or asking the head nurse

for a blanket even while I lay shivering
on a gurney with an IV in my arm.
Helpless and restrained, I saw a father

who made no move to stop an incensed mother
from feeding their colicky baby – sick
of raising a bottle to my mouth, she

dropped me into the cradle from a height
of four feet. After twenty years, he told me
how he called the cops who could do nothing,

all on record in a box somewhere. I love
men who still wear uniforms sewn with care
by women expert with needle and thread.

Where is she who mended mountains of clothes
that do not fit me now? Who is that man
who weeps unheard inside my body? I love men

who do not raise their voices in a crowd
even when they are moving in the wrong
direction – men who were never loved, I love.

POEM

If I held back each word, perhaps
there would be peace instead
of an open suitcase on the bed.
Or a broken bottle of gin
pooling on the kitchen floor.
Things as they were. No thought
of a silver wedding knife
buried somewhere in the yard.
Or was that just another lie
my mother told as grief hovered
over us – not a jet engine
so high we could barely hear it
but a thin trail of exhaust
dissolving across the evening sky.

SHE SMASHES DISHES

My mother climbing into bed,
me not sleeping. Death waits

outside, lighting a cigarette.
He glances down at a watch

that has no hands. *Soon, soon,*
he thinks, then takes another

drag. Me slipping out of bed
at dawn to pick up the pieces.

APOSTASY

We open our mouths and the seasons
change, screech owls lifting mice
into the sky those starless hours
when schools of fish are darting
under windows made of ice. Oh Christ
in the chords of an old harmonica
held up to a child's mouth, a solemn
hymn whose words we dare not sing.

NAKED

1. What Starts as a Gesture Between Us

One moment we lie in a meadow
listening to the wind, and the next
    we are lost in a forest

of fallen needles. Even when birds
are out of sight, we cannot stop
    the singing. It's late summer

and I walk into the coldest room
of the house. You wait in the garden,
    break an iris off its stalk

then set it in a bowl of water.
In that quiet, the space between us
    changes into music. An ant

emerges from the flower's chamber,
inching its way to the petal's edge
    then turns back. You look at me

but I no longer can hear your voice
as I take the flower and thrust it
    all the way into my mouth.

2. *A View of the Garden*

Do we need alibis? I broke the vase
into four rivers, forgive me.
By the brook, a sweet theatrical rose.
Loud. Distracted. A coil lounging
near the grass, the slow unwinding day –

What had been forbidden
transformed us: a mouth-shaped abyss
opened all around us, the sky
framing absence where a voice had been,
the voice of God, you said –

What reawakens is but a muted cry
to the choirs that shook those bowers
where we had slept. No singing now,
only that endless ticking
from a clock we cannot silence.

3. Cycling

I will look for you in roadside
flowers, in the shifting gears

as I cycle across the bridge,
your odor in the steel, the sweat

streaking down my back. It is not
your body that I remember best

but pulling up the sheet to cover
our faces. Or finding a watch

that fell behind the bed. Then
that pulsing pain as we regained

a sense of time. I leave your side –
another comes to take my place.

4. *Evening Song*

Our voices entangled on a single bed,
so hard to tell apart. I miss
your neck, the floral sheets a garden
where I awoke alone.
Last summer, I swallowed your seed
and a tree took root inside,
flesh of my flesh, bone of your bone,
but paradise was more than us:
a key that melted when I returned
to what I no longer owned – your bed
a revolving door, our world a dusk rose
closing, evening a cricket playing
the one song that it knows.

5. *White Blossoms*

Does your face still shine when you speak
my Chinese name? If I told you
three apricots have fallen to the ground
where we once walked, that I ate
bruised flesh and blessed each pit,
that trinity, would you believe
an orchard has taken root inside of me
even as I speak, each character
carved into the bark by your own hand?

6. Storm Warning

Star charts have no meaning for us now.
In that photo where you leave no shadow –
a night on asphalt glistening with rain,
the taste of whiskey on your kisses
that held me there. Everything as it was,
the two of us at Memorial Park, running
side-by-side until I took the lead.
It's true we met at the finish
but something was lost that hour:
the clouds closing in, a neon sign
blinking off and on, each gesture
a measure of all our failures.
Whenever it rains, I lift my mouth
to the sky and your street floods over,
a car up to its doors in water, trousers
drying on a chair. How happy we were
bailing out the backseat, wondering
if the engine would start again.
The last time I saw you, your hair
was a lighter shade, more buoyant, and I
envied the sun, the visible changes
my absence had made more apparent.
What are words that I should live in them
and sing of your love for me
even in our silence? *Ask for anything*,
you once said in a world
with windows darkening. What could I say,
everything I wanted right there.

7. *What Is Left Behind*

Two pieces of toast with marmalade on top,
sticky crumbs that fall into the cracks
of my keyboard, an oscillating fan
the only source of white noise in this house.
A pack of unsharpened pencils with your name
on each, its lead beginnings – shavings
spiraling off the steel blade like apple peel –
all those reams of recycled paper
stacked up like laundered shirts. What happened
to those porcelain birds from China or the slides
we never viewed – dim sum in Tsim Sha Tsui
then up to the Peak? You took my key
and drove away, not knowing where you were.
You like your coffee black. There's sugar
on the table, no spoon, a carton of half-
and-half almost twelve days past its date.
There's a bedroom window you left open.
If only you were here. If only you
could hear me typing anything but this.

8. Naked

Not a single piece of furniture between us.
No car. No radio. No road. Only this music
on a cheap cassette I stash in the glove box,
a tape I have played over seventy times.
You could have given me something that lasted
longer, cost more, like a Sunday afternoon
at the zoo. Or a Hindemith sonata. Before
I changed the outgoing message on my machine.
Only my voice remains the same. No duets.
Nothing like the two of us in a supermarket
with a bottle of tonic water that had the wrong
price on it. We were thirsty, but it was you
who said, *I think of you naked all the time.*
Outside the sculpture-garden gates, a viola
worth a hundred thousand dollars in the trunk
of your car. Whatever led us to the shade
of a live oak made me ask if you would share
a fantasy you had about my body, and you said,
it's none of your business. In that garden,
Giacometti's woman standing larger-than-life
and a triptych of Matisse in bronze relief,
that study of a woman's back losing its hold
on reality, frame by frame, her body itself
dissolving into pure form. It is almost Sunday.

9. A World Made out of Absence

No news from you, only the voice of Whitman
on the radio last night – a recording
Edison had saved on a cylinder made of wax,
discovered after all these years. *Timing
is everything*, a woman once said, she
who had waited twenty years to spend one night
with a man in Vermont. Those woods. That bed
of Queen Anne's lace just off the road
will never be ours. Nor that room in Houston
where you slept (a stranger's bathrobe
draped on a chair), me in Philadelphia
on Locust and Eighteenth, tracing those steps
where you had been fifteen years before,
viola at your side as you disappeared
behind that stone façade of Curtis Institute.
Why call late at night just to hear a voice
recorded on some machine, as if words
could make distances retreat? Driving home
on the Pike, I wonder if I am present
in a landscape where you have never been.

Against our will. A few words. An afternoon.
I told the custodian I had locked myself out.
He led me through a soundproof door, then left me

sitting there behind your desk – cleared at last
of clutter. What we would cram into those minutes
between students, sheet music pushed to the floor.

Face up, face down, everything I thought I knew
was altered. One day, the clock behind us vanished,
leaving a tiny metal hook halfway up the wall.

Later it was Chagall's *The Woman and the Roses*
hanging there. Nothing in that studio mattered
except when I was in it (you once said), my head

in your lap as you whispered over and over,
Questa o quella per me pari sono. Why then return?
Even roses drop their petals when no one's here

but that woman reclined on a rosebush framed
behind glass will outlast what we had, asking
for nothing, only that you leave her as she is.

ACROSS THE RIVER

A steady wind. A childhood
that waits for us as daffodils
shed their husks on a shore
where no one has wept for years.
There is another world, time
enough for walks, for testimonies
of wood in a cast-iron stove.
A decrescendo. A wilderness
on fire. Then rain. Finally snow
with no one's footprints in it.

BENEDICTION

What lies buried under six feet of snow
waits to be found while a candle on the sill

burns down, flame guttering over a pool
of wax that hardens when an intimate mouth

comes to extinguish it. How pages of a Bible
keep turning in our sleep while children

ascend the winding stair with prayers long
forgotten. What lingers on in memory returns

as a dream unscrolled, the images most dear
to us nothing more than a blind flickering

on an hourglass near empty. It is no wonder
a candle burns perpetual behind our backs

even as we stare out past a sea of snow
where the voices of what we were converge

with what we are – incorruptible shadows
that sink back down to the depths below.

BOOK DESIGN by John D. Berry. Composition by Typeworks. The type is Janson Text, a digital adaptation by Adrian Frutiger of the 17th-century type of Hungarian punch-cutter Nicholas Kis. Kis spent ten years working in Amsterdam, and his type is one of the sturdy old-style type-faces typical of Dutch printing of the period. In the 20th century, it was adapted for hot-metal composition and widely used in fine books. The revived typeface was called "Janson" because it was mistakenly attributed at first to Anton Janson, a Dutch typographer who worked in Leipzig. Janson Text retains many of the idiosyncracies of the original design and maintains its legibility at text sizes.